Tyler's Titanic

Tyler's Titanic

Bernard Ryan, Jr.

RDR Books
Oakland, California

4456 Piedmont
Oakland, CA 94611
Phone: (510) 595-0595
Fax: (510) 595-0598
E-mail: read@rdrbooks.com
Website: www.rdrbooks.com

ISBN 1-57143-085-7
Library of Congress Control Number 2001095684

Editor: Martha Jackson
Cover Design: Paula Morrison
Text Design and Typography: Richard Harris
Proofreader: Joanna Pearlman

Distributed in the United Kingdom and Europe by
Roundhouse Publishing, Ltd.
Millstone, Limers Lane
Northam, Devon EX39 2RG
United Kingdom

Distributed in Canada by
Starbooks Distribution
100 Armstrong Way
Georgetown, ON L7G 5S4

Printed in Canada

for
Tyler Joseph Johnson
and his sister
Anna Eames Johnson

CONTENTS

1. Getting Ready 9
2. Arriving at the Seashore 19
3. Dipping Up the Ocean 25
4. Calling for Tyler 31
5. Finding the *Titanic* 37
6. Climbing Aboard the Wreck . . .43
7. Meeting Captain Smith 50
8. Discovering the Dogs 57
9. Meeting the Kids 65
10. Playing the CD 72
11. Beating Down Demons 78
12. Following the Dogs 84
13. Facing the Crowd 93
    Author's Note on Sources 95
    Titanic Facts 100

CHAPTER 1

Getting Ready

IT WAS FRIDAY AFTERNOON. Tyler's mom stood at the foot of the stairs. "Tyler?"

No answer.

"*Ty*-ler!" she called.

Still no answer.

She started up the stairs. Halfway up, she heard his voice.

"Mom! I'm on the Internet. I'm just in the middle of . . ."

She stopped at the door of his room. "You're not supposed to be on the Internet. You're supposed to be packing."

"I *am* packing. But I had to find some stuff."

She looked over his shoulder at the computer. "What kind of stuff?"

"There's a book I don't have," said Tyler without turning around. "Look. It's on Amazon. I can get it for . . . "

"Another *Titanic* book? Yet another?"

"It's got the pictures from the wreck."

"You already have pictures from the wreck."

"No, these are the new ones. From the videoscan. They're the best color shots yet. I can order it right from . . . "

Tyler's mother sat down. "Look. I thought you were packing your gear for this trip. I find you searching Amazon for still more books. I've got a million things to do if we're going to get to the shore before dark tomorrow. I've got to get your sister's things ready, too."

"But that's it," said Tyler. "If I order it now, it'll be here when we get back."

"Besides," said his mother, "I've told you a hundred times, we're not spending another penny on *Titanic* books. That whole subject is all over. Nobody's talking about the *Titanic* any more. Nobody's even thinking about it."

"I am," said Tyler. "I think about it all the time. It's number one in my head. All the time."

"Tell you what," said Mom. "You tell your ten-year-old head to get busy packing. Then maybe we'll talk."

"I *am* busy packing. I just stopped for a few minutes, just a couple of minutes."

Mom stood up. "You get everything packed. Your swim stuff, shorts, shoes, videotapes, CDs, and books."

"Mom!"

"Everything we talked about taking for a week at the seashore, get it all together, ready to put in the car. Then you check out Bibliomation. See if the library has the book. If they have it, you can call your friend. What's her name? Mrs. Bannister."

"The library?"

"Ask her to hold it for you. I'll run you

down there so you can pick it up this afternoon, soon as Dad gets home. Okay?"

Tyler smiled. "Okay."

"But I mean it. Packing first. Your father expects you to have things ready to load in the car when he gets home."

"Mom, I know."

"That's a long trip tomorrow. We'll be on the road just about all day. We need an early start."

"Well, then, see?" said Tyler. "That's a good reason to have a new *Titanic* book to read in the car."

"Which is why it's a good idea to get it from the library before we go," said his mother, "not from Amazon when we get back."

"But if it's good, I'll want to get it for my collection."

"We'll see," said his mother over her shoulder as she stepped back into the hallway. "Pack. Now. All your stuff. Neat and orderly."

"Ohhh-kay," said Tyler.

She was in his doorway again. "And another thing. Where's Spoofer? Isn't it time you took him out?"

"Right here," said Tyler. "He's under the bed. He isn't asking to go out."

"If I know that dog, I know he's ready to go out," said Tyler's mother. "Now get packing. And take Spoofer out."

"Which first?"

"Don't exasperate me, Tyler. Give that dog his walk. And get yourself together. And your gear. Okay?"

NOW IT WAS LATE FRIDAY AFTERNOON. Spoofer had had his walk. Tyler was back in his room and his Dad was in his doorway. "What's this about getting a book from the library?"

"Mom said she'd take me," said Tyler. "It's that new book about the *Titanic*."

"Do they have it?"

"I called. Mrs. Bannister said she'll hold it for me."

"C'mon," said his Dad. "Your mom's got more than enough to do."

"Can I go?" came a voice from the next room.

"Sure," said Tyler's Dad. "But come on. We're leaving right now."

"That Anna," said Tyler. "Why does she have to go?"

"You know she never misses a trip in the car."

"Yeah," said Tyler, "she always wants to go with me. Why can't I go someplace without my four-year-old sister tagging along?"

"I'm almost five," said the voice from the next room. "Daddy, tell him I'm almost five. I'm almost five, Tyler."

THE THREE OF THEM were in the car. "Another *Titanic* book, huh?" said Tyler's Dad.

"It's the best one yet," said Tyler. "It's that last expedition. All those color shots. They're really great. It's like you're . . . "

"Like you're right down there?"

"Yeah. Yeah, Dad, you can just feel it."

"Isn't that what you said when you saw that TV show? The one you videotaped?"

"The one on the History Channel," said Tyler. "That was cool. But this is different."

"How?"

"Well, actually, because it's still pictures. You can really study them. All the closeups of the decks and the railings and everything. And all the stuff lying around on the floor of the ocean."

"I didn't like it," said Anna.

"You didn't?" said her Dad.

"Too scary."

"You didn't have to look," said Tyler.

"I did so. You had it on the TV."

"Nobody made you watch."

"I don't think you saw too much of it, Anna," said Dad. "I think that was the time you went upstairs. You said your Barbies didn't want to see all that old stuff."

"Yeah," said Tyler. "You picked up three Barbies and took them with you. You said the bottom of the ocean was a stupid place."

Tyler paused a moment. Anna was

looking out the window. "Besides, Dad," Tyler went on, "if this book's as good as they say it is, I can add it to my collection."

"Y'know, Tyler," said his Dad, "your collection is kind of getting out of hand. Your closet is bursting with *Titanic* this and *Titanic* that. In fact, your whole room is."

"But Dad, it's my collection."

"One of these days, it's going to crowd us right out of the house. From the day you saw that movie, it's been one *Titanic* thing after another. The movie videotape. All those other videos. How many have you got? Every TV interview. The CDs. The books."

Tyler smiled. "Mrs. Bannister says I must be an expert by now."

"Is that what she said? When did she say that?"

"When I called. About the book. She says I'm the town's best *Titanic* expert."

"She may just be right," said Dad. "But you know what?"

"What?"

"You know, Tyler, you really have to think about moving on to something else. You can't just spend your whole life, month in, month out, year in, year out, being an expert on the *Titanic*."

"Why not?" said Tyler. "Why can't I? I'm not just going to be the town's best expert. I'm going to be the world's best expert. Mister Titanic, they'll call me."

"Mister Titanic?"

"Professor Titanic," said Tyler. "Maybe even Doctor Titanic. Spoofer and me, we're the experts, Dad. Spoofer's always with me when I'm on the *Titanic*. He knows as much as I know. Maybe more."

"When you're *on* the *Titanic*?"

Tyler grinned. "Well, that's what Tom said."

"Tom?"

"Tom Taylor. He said, 'Oh, you're always on the *Titanic*.'"

"When did he say that?"

"When he came over. Yesterday."

"Well," said Dad, "why'd he say that? What were you doing?"

"He had this new Zelda game he wanted to play. And I was surfing the Internet for new *Titanic* stuff. So I didn't want to log out of that and play his game. You know, Nintendo's always got some new game."

"Well, you want to think about that, Tyler," said Dad. "Do all your friends think you're always on the *Titanic*?"

Tyler shrugged. "I don't know. They're used to me. I don't know."

"Well, think about it. You can't just turn your friends on and off, you know."

They stopped in the library parking lot. "Okay, Doctor Titanic," said Dad. "Hop in there and get your book. And don't dawdle. I want this car loaded before dinner."

CHAPTER 2

Arriving at the Seashore

THE DRIVE TO THE SEASHORE seemed to have taken all day. But it was still only mid-afternoon as Tyler and his father finished unloading the car. Now they stood beside the cottage, gazing across the dunes. The brilliant sun warmed their backs. The surf foamed up gently in a line along the beach, then slid back into the green-brown sea. Far off, deep green waves met the bluest sky Tyler had ever seen. And here came Spoofer racing back toward them from way down the beach. His nose grazed the packed sand and his ears flip-flapped as he sniffed his way along.

"It's all yours," said Dad. "Your Atlantic. Yours and Anna's. For all this week. Here, can you put this last bag somewhere?"

"That's Anna's stuff," said Tyler. "Where's Anna?"

"She's too little to carry a bag that big," said his father.

Tyler stretched his arms around the big canvas bag. He lugged it into the cottage. "Hey, Mom, where does this go?"

"Just put it on that chair by the bathroom door," called Mom from the kitchen. She was busy checking out the pots and pans in the drawer under the stove. "Hmmm," she murmured. "Some people's idea of what you need in a kitchen."

"Hey, Sal," called Dad from the door, "I'm going to drive over to the harbor. I want to see if Captain Wilton can take us on his cruise tomorrow. We'll catch some blues for dinner."

"Good idea," said Mom.

"Want to come, Ty?" called Dad.

"I can't find my boom box," said Tyler from his room. "No. I'll stay here. Who's got my boom box?"

"Did you bring it in?" said Mom.

"Wait!" yelled Tyler. He dashed out to the car. There it was on the back seat, right where he had had it between Anna and himself the whole trip.

Dad was standing with the car door open. One foot was already in the car. "Hey, Anna!" he called. "You want to go with me?"

Anna came around from the front deck of the cottage. In one hand she held her bright yellow plastic shovel, the handle of her bright red plastic bucket in the other. "I want to make a sand castle," she said.

"Okay," said Dad. "But the sand's too dry up here by the house. You'll have to go down by the water. You need wet sand to make castles."

Anna turned and headed back toward the front of the house and the broad stretch of sand and beach grass beyond it.

"Wait a minute," called her father.

"You can't go down there by yourself. Tyler, you keep an eye on your sister."

"Dad!"

"Just for a few minutes. I won't be long. Anna, you wait for Tyler."

"Oh, all right," said Anna. "But does he have to bring that stupid boom box?"

"Tyler, you keep it down low," said Dad. "I'm out of here."

Tyler headed into the cottage with his boom box. "Where's my bag of stuff?" he asked as he passed the kitchen.

"I would guess it's wherever you put it in your room," said Mom. "What are you looking for?"

"I want my *Titanic* tape."

"Tyler, come back here," said Mom from the kitchen.

He turned to the kitchen. Mom was kneeling on the floor in front of the stove. All around her were pots and pans. In her hand was a rusty frying pan. "Tyler," she said, "you are not going to play that three-hour video on the very first afternoon of our vacation on a lovely summer day like this."

"I just want to check out the VCR," said Tyler. "What if it doesn't work?"

"We'll find that out later. Your father and I told you before we left home. All videos, including *Titanic*, are for rainy days and after dark. It is not dark yet and it is certainly not raining."

"Just to see if it works?" Tyler pleaded.

"No. And besides, you've seen *Titanic* at the movies more times than anybody else in the world. And you've run that video so many times it's a wonder it isn't worn right through. You can check the VCR after dinner."

"Mom!"

"I mean it," she said. "Now. Out on the beach. Didn't I hear your father tell you to keep an eye on Anna? She's dying to play in the sand. Take Spoofer. He could use a good run. Get some of this sea breeze and sunshine. Find some kids your age. You might run into somebody who's been here a while."

"Why don't you come?" asked Tyler.

"I've got too much to do to get this place in shape so we can have a nice vacation. Just look at this." She held up the rusty frying pan. "All the pots and pans in this cottage look as if they came from the wreck of the *Titanic* itself. Want to help shine them up?"

"I guess I'll go out with Spoofer and Anna," said Tyler. He picked up his boom box.

"You're taking that?" said his mother.

"Sure. If I can't watch *Titanic,* I can at least listen to it."

"You played that CD twice on the ride down here," said Mom. "You must know it by heart."

"I do," said Tyler.

"So do I," she said. "I feel like I've heard nothing else for months. Now, out. Take your pail. Help your sister build a castle. Find me some pretty shells. Big ones, to put on the windowsill here. This place needs some atmosphere. And not too loud on the beach. People are here to relax. They're not dying to hear your boom box."

CHAPTER 3

Dipping Up the Ocean

SPOOFER BARKED AT A SEA GULL. He chased after it down the beach. Then, his nose sniffing the sand, he ran back toward where Tyler was sitting and Anna was packing wet sand into a big block.

Suddenly Spoofer stopped. He sniff-sniffed. His ears flicked in the sand. He began to dig. His paws spun round and round. The sand flew out behind him.

He stopped and looked up, first at Anna, then at Tyler, then back again at Anna. He cocked his head to one side. He barked.

Anna went closer. Spoofer crouched down. His front paws were deep in the hole he had dug. His tail wagged back and forth as he yip-yipped at Anna. He ran to the edge of the water, his front paws splashing as a gentle wave washed toward him. He looked back at Anna and barked again.

"You like the ocean, don't you, Spoof?" said Tyler, gazing far out where the sea met the sky.

Spoofer dashed back to them. He turned and sat beside Tyler. Tyler patted his head. "It's out there, Spoof," he said quietly. "It's way out there. Way, way out there. You know it, don't you? And deep. Way down deep, too."

He put his arm around the dog, cradling Spoofer's head against his chest. Spoofer squirmed loose and ran again to the edge of the water, splashing as a wave rolled in.

"What do you want?" asked Tyler.

Spoofer came bouncing back to the hole. He jumped in and dug hard. The sand flew out behind him. And now he ran yippety–yappety to the water again.

"You want us to put some water in the hole?" said Tyler. "Hey, Anna, you know what? I think Spoofer wants water in that hole."

Anna picked up her bucket. She ran to the edge of the ocean. As the next wave rolled in, she dipped up some water. Spoofer scampered along beside her. Anna took her bucketful of water and dumped it in the hole.

Spoofer watched the water disappear into the sand. When it was all gone, he yelped again and ran back to the edge of the ocean.

Anna dipped up another bucketful of water. She poured it into the hole. Down it went. Spoofer ran in a happy circle around the hole. His tail kept wagging. He was yipping and yapping and yelping all the way. Now he was back at the water's edge. His body crouched down onto his front paws. His rear legs were stiff and straight. His rear end wagged back and forth with his tail.

Anna looked at Spoofer. Then she turned to where Tyler was sitting on the sand. "I know what he wants," she said.

"What?" said Tyler.

"He wants me to put more water in the hole."

"Yeah?" said Tyler.

"He wants me to put the whole ocean in the hole."

"Don't be stupid," said Tyler. "You can't put the whole ocean in that hole."

"Yes, I can," said Anna. "Spoofer knows." She ran down the beach. "Spoofer knows I can."

Anna dipped up another bucketful. She poured it in the hole. Spoofer ran beside her. Anna kept on dipping and pouring. Spoofer kept on scampering back and forth, crouching at the hole, watching the water disappear, begging for more.

THE SUN WAS LOW, shining across the tops of the dunes. Dad came along. "Supper!" he called out. "Tyler! Anna! Come to supper!"

"Busy!" yelled Anna.

Her father looked down. He saw Anna dumping a bucket of water into the hole. He saw her watch it sink into the sand. "What are you doing, Anna?"

"I'm putting the ocean in this hole," said Anna. "Spoofer dug this hole. He asked me to dump water in it. I'm going to dump the whole ocean in."

"You are?" asked Dad.

"It's a very deep hole," said Anna. "It's going to take the whole ocean to fill it up." She hurried back to the edge of the sea.

"Won't it take quite a while?" said her father.

"No," said Anna. "Look how much I did already. The ocean was way up here when I started." She pointed along the beach where strands of seaweed and bits of driftwood and seashells made a wavy line.

"And then what?" called Dad as she headed back toward the water's edge. "What happens when you've dumped all that water into the hole?"

"I don't know," said Anna. "Tyler said if I do it he's going to go see the *Titanic*."

"Where is Tyler?" said her father.

"He took a walk."

"And where's Spoofer?"

"With Tyler," said Anna.

She pointed far off down the beach. "They're walking down that way," she said, "with that stupid boom box."

CHAPTER 4

Calling for Tyler

DAD WENT BACK to the cottage. "I'm not going to make an issue, our first night here," he said to Mom. "They're having a good time. Anna's all alone out there."

"What do you mean, Anna's all alone out there?"

"She's playing in the sand. She's fine. And she has this crazy idea."

"You mean to tell me," said Mom, "that boy left his four-year-old sister alone on the beach? Where is he?"

"He's up the beach somewhere," said

31

Dad. "He just went for a walk on the beach. Anna saw him go."

"Anna saw him go? You mean now she's the one keeping an eye on the other one? That little girl's guarding her big brother?"

"Oh, come on, Sal," said Dad. "They can't go anywhere. And they'll come in when they get hungry."

"And Spoofer?" asked Mom. "I suppose that dog's gone off in some other direction."

"Anna said he's with Tyler. You know Spoofer. He never goes anywhere by himself."

"You want to bet?" said Mom. "You know what happens when he finds other dogs to chase around with. We won't see him for hours."

"He isn't chasing off with anybody. Anna saw him with Tyler."

"And just what on earth is Anna doing down there by herself?"

"She's trudging back and forth between a hole in the sand and the edge of the water. She's dipping up water and pouring it in a hole. She says she's going to dump the whole ocean into it. She can show you how much the ocean has already gone down. I hate to tell her it's just because the tide went out."

"Whatever gave her that idea?" asked Mom.

"I don't know. She said something about Spoofer digging a hole, as she put it. And he wanted her to pour the ocean into it. And you know that Anna."

"I know. The most determined four-year-old in town, as you always say."

"You haven't heard the best part," said Dad. "Anna says Tyler told her if she pours the whole ocean into that hole in the sand, he's going to hike out to the *Titanic*."

"The wreck?"

"Yup," said Dad. "And you know what gave him *that* idea."

Anna walked in. "I'm hungry!"

"Look at that bucket," said Dad. "That's a tired bucket."

"It's not tired," said Anna. "What's for dinner?"

"Well, its sides are all scraped," said Dad. "It's not the nice bright red it was when we got here."

"The sand did that," said Anna. "I had to drag it over the sand. That's how I got water for the hole."

"Anna," said Mom, "there's crackers and cheese on the table. And you can have some milk. That'll hold you until dinner."

"When's dinner?" said Anna.

"When Tyler comes in," said Mom. "And where is your brother? And Spoofer? Where's Spoofer?"

"I don't know. Tyler said he was going for a long walk. He said he was going so far away I wouldn't even hear his dumb boom box. Spoofer likes the boom box. He doesn't care. I hate it."

ANNA AND HER MOTHER AND FATHER had munched on crackers and cheese. Now the sun was beginning to set. "Notice how quiet it is?" said Dad to Mom. "I guess the wind's died down. I don't think there's any surf at all."

"I'm going out and get that boy," said

Mom. "He must be exhausted. And we're all starving."

Dad and Anna stood on the front deck of the cottage and watched Mom hurry up to the top of the dune. She disappeared down the side toward the ocean. They could hear her calling, "Ty-y-y-ler! Ty-y-y-ler!"

But now her voice changed. "Jim!" she called back. She sounded afraid. "Jim! Hurry! Jim! Hurry!"

Dad dashed up the path through the beach grass to the top of the dune. Mom stood far down the slope. "Look!" she said. "Just look! Look at this!"

In the growing twilight, the beach sloped down and down and down. It stretched for miles before them, a broad, flat valley of pink and yellow sand. Far, far away, tiny puddles and little ponds and lakes were shining here and there. Among them grew forests of seaweed, blue-green and red-brown. Overhead, a few stars were beginning to sparkle in the deep blue sky. Far in the east, the full moon was rising.

Tyler's Mom and Dad gazed to the left. They gazed to the right. They looked and looked for the hole Spoofer had dug. They called for Spoofer and they called for Tyler.

Nobody answered. Nobody came.

CHAPTER 5

Finding the *Titanic*

TYLER HIKED ALONG. The farther he walked, the easier it seemed to be and the lighter his boom box felt. He kept it playing softly. The moon was big and full and bright silver. It made enough light so Tyler could see Spoofer running far ahead.

As they hiked along, the moon had moved across the sky. And now, standing before them was a huge dark shape.

It was like a great black wall. Tyler moved closer. Lights, millions of lights, seemed to be flickering softly behind the dark wall. Is it? he wondered. Is it the *Titanic*?

The soft sand flowed up toward an opening in the wall. The opening was round but framed by jagged rusty shapes that looked like icicles. Spoofer jumped up, putting his front paws on the edge of the opening. His tail was wagging so hard it was almost a blur.

Through the opening, Tyler saw something move. Spoofer barked. Tyler heard a voice. "Come in here, young man."

Tyler moved closer and put his arm around Spoofer's neck. They peered into the rusty opening. Now he could see the face of a man with curly black hair. He had deep-set dark eyes and was grinning at Tyler, a tooth missing just at the left corner of his mouth. "Come in, lad. Come aboard."

"I can't get through this hole," said Tyler.

"Just push on in. That's a good lad." The voice was deep and calm.

"I can't."

"Then I'll step ashore meself," said the voice.

Tyler stepped back as the face came

toward the hole. Spoofer dropped down onto all fours. Now a misty shape appeared outside the rusty dark wall. Tyler stepped farther back. The shape became a man, all in black. A tight-fitting black shirt like a thick, heavy T-shirt. But no sleeves. Wide shoulders and thick, strong arms dark with sooty black splotches. Black pants heavier than jeans. Thick twine tied around each leg just below the knee, so the pants pulled up away from heavy, black boots.

"How did you do that?" asked Tyler.

"Do what, lad?"

"Come through the wall that way. How could you?"

The man crouched, his hands on his knees. He leaned toward Tyler's face. "I do what any spirit can do, lad. I just take a deep breath and put me nose up against whatever I want to go through."

He turned to the wall. "See? Nose first. Them as is here forever, lad," he said, his husky voice barely louder than a whisper, "we just push against the solids. And through we go."

With that, the man took a step and dissolved into the wall.

"Wait!" called Tyler.

The man appeared again, stepping back toward Tyler and Spoofer. "I must say," he said, "it makes things a lot easier than when I was alive. You haven't tried it yet?"

"You're a ghost?" asked Tyler.

"Now, lad. That's not a word we like around here," said the man. "A spirit, yes. A spirit."

"Who are you the spirit of?" asked Tyler.

"Of meself. George Kemish, fireman, *Titanic* night crew, boiler room four. And yourself? You're the spirit of?

"Nobody," said Tyler. "I'm not a spirit. I'm alive. I can't walk through anything solid."

Fireman Kemish straightened up. Slowly he strolled around Tyler and Spoofer, looking them over. When he had made a complete circle, he spoke. "Not a spirit. In the real world, eh? That's it?"

"Yes."

"And you go by the name of?"

"Tyler."

"Tyler," said Kemish. "Good British name. Well, Tyler, can you explain something?" The fireman paused.

"What?"

Kemish leaned forward again. His hands were on his knees. His eyes were popping wide open. His voice was husky as he almost whispered a question. "What's become of the sea?"

"My sister poured it in a hole," said Tyler.

"Your sister poured it in a hole?"

"In the beach," said Tyler. "Spoofer dug this hole, and he wanted her to . . . "

"Spoofer?" said fireman Kemish.

"My dog. He's Spoofer. And my sister, her name is Anna, she just kept dipping up water and pouring it in this hole."

"I see," said Kemish, sounding as if he did not quite understand. He looked at Tyler, then at Spoofer, then back at Tyler. "I'll ask you one more question."

"Okay," said Tyler.

The fireman leaned toward Tyler again. "What is it I keep hearing? Afar off, it seems. But nearby, too. A strange sound. Sometimes a voice. Do you hear it?"

"Sure," said Tyler.

"Is it music, do you think?"

"Sure," said Tyler again. "It's my boom box." And he picked it up and turned up the volume.

The fireman jumped backward. "Oh, me! Oh, me! What a blitherin' noise! Me ears! Oh, me ears!"

Tyler turned down the sound.

"Your boom box, eh?" said the fireman. "How does it make that noise?"

"It's a radio," said Tyler.

"Radio, then?" repeated Kemish. "The wireless, is it?"

"I guess so," said Tyler.

The fireman turned toward the great dark wall. "Come along with me. I know a spirit who'll want to hear that boom box. Come along, lad. I'll show you where to get aboard."

CHAPTER 6

Climbing Aboard the Wreck

TYLER PICKED UP HIS BOOM BOX and followed fireman Kemish alongside the great wall. Spoofer scampered beside him. Soon they came to a jagged opening. A bent piece of the ship's railing shone in the moonlight.

"See, lad," said Kemish, "see how the brass still shines. The currents in the sea do that, you know. Not everything is rot and rust. The sea, lad. The sea shines up the brass."

Now they climbed. Up stairs so tilted Tyler thought he couldn't make his way.

Spoofer jumped ahead, then turned, his head cocked to the side, looking back as Tyler caught up with him. Fireman Kemish led them, stair after stair. They crossed great slanting decks. Tyler peered into vast rooms. They were filled with broken chairs and pianos and tables and scattered plates and cups and saucers. Bits and pieces of china and glass were mixed with whole, unbroken platters and pitchers and lamps. But some lights still hung from the ceiling, and they were brightly lighted. And far down the hallways they passed, lights flickered here and there.

At last they stopped climbing. "Boat deck," said Kemish, as if that was all he had to say about where they were. "Come along."

The deck was like walking along the side of a hill without going upward or downward. To the left, the brass of the railing shone brightly. To the right, the cabin wall stood with great gashes where its seams had burst open. Light shone through.

Spoofer zig-zagged up and down the slope. Tyler and Kemesh stepped over wires that drooped in their path from metal poles bent in crazy directions. Here and there, as they moved along, they had to step over rusted orange blobs of metal.

Kemish stopped at a door that hung by only one hinge. It belonged to a doorway that was all out of shape. It was squashed down at the top and its sides slanted to the left.

"Wireless shack," said Kemish. "And here's first operator Phillips."

"What's this, then?" said a voice from somewhere inside.

"Visitor," said Kemish. "Come out on deck, Phillips."

Through the wall came a figure. It seemed made of mist, as if it would clear away if you blew on it. As it stepped toward him, Tyler could still see the wall through the shape of a man. Now it was more solid. Was the man wearing earphones? Yes. Now Tyler could see big earphones. They were black, with shiny metal frames holding them and a black cord dangling from each. The cords connected in front of the man's chest, over a thick, bulging, khaki-colored canvas shape. A life-jacket. The man's arms, reaching out from the shoulders of the life-jacket, wore black sleeves with dingy gold braid at the cuffs. His uniform, thought Tyler.

"A visitor?" the man was saying.

"With a boom box," said Kemish. "Tyler, me lad, first operator Phillips is in charge of the wireless."

"The Marconi, we call it," said Phillips. "Young man, how do you do?"

A strong arm reached out to shake Tyler's hand. "Boom box? Do I know that word? Do I know what that is, lad?"

"Make it boom," said Kemish.

Tyler turned up the volume. A steady hard beat rattled the loose boards. The door that was hanging by a hinge began to vibrate.

"That's a boom," said Phillips. "Boom enough, I'd say. It's the new-fangled wireless, I expect. Must it be so loud?"

Tyler turned it down.

Phillips looked at fireman Kemish. "A Marconi he carries about with him. And no earphones. What have we come to?"

"It works with earphones," said Tyler.

"Does it, now?" said Phillips. He bent over the boom box, grasping the end of the wire that hung down in front of his chest. "Let me try it."

"Here," said Tyler, pointing to the small hole at the back of the boom box. "Plug it in here."

Phillips plugged in his earphones. "Not too loud, there, Tyler," he said. "I'll keep my eardrums unbroken, thank you."

Phillips listened for a moment. His eyes brightened. His broad smile burst into a grin. "That Marconi," he said at last. "Sheer genius, I'd say. Here, Kemish. Give a listen."

He pulled the earphones off his head and clapped them onto the fireman's head. Kemish grinned and nodded. He pulled off the earphones. "The sound is all in the middle of me head," he said. "Here, lad, you try it." He put them onto Tyler's head.

"I'm used to it," said Tyler. He pulled the earphones from his ears and let them drop down around his neck. "My Mom makes me use earphones whenever I play it too loud."

"And where are your earphones?" asked Phillips.

"Home," said Tyler. "With my stuff."

"Then take these," said Phillips. "You'll need them. Folks hereabouts don't expect to hear boom boxes."

"But they're yours," said Tyler.

"I have more," said Phillips. "Second operator Bride left his at his post. And we have more in the supply cabinet. We sailed well equipped. Eh, Kemish?"

"That we did," said Kemish, nodding.

"I should think the captain would like to know about this," said Phillips.

"About the boom box?" said Kemish.

"And the boy," said Phillips. "The captain will want to check the passenger list."

Kemish shook his head. "He's not on it," he said. "This lad's not a spirit from the list. He's flesh and blood. He scooped up the sea."

Phillips stepped back. "You, lad? You scooped up the sea?"

"My sister poured it in a hole," said Tyler. "Spoofer dug a hole."

"Spoofer?" said Phillips.

"The dog," said Kemish. "The lad brought the dog along."

"The dog's not a spirit, then?" asked Phillips.

"He's alive," said Tyler. "Like me."

Phillips nodded slowly. "Dog and boom box and a quick young lad," he said. "Himself will want to know about this. We'd best get to the bridge." He turned and started along the deck.

CHAPTER 7

Meeting Captain Smith

WITHIN A FEW STEPS, the deck ended. Tyler could look down toward the bow of the wreck. They turned right and climbed up the slope. Now Tyler saw an old man who was quietly watching them come toward him. He wore a white beard. His cap was white on top, above a black band that went round his head, its visor encrusted with tarnished metal. His white jacket was closed tightly by a large metal button where its collar stood up under his beard. Black shapes like flaps atop each shoulder were decorated with tarnished metal. The cuffs of his jacket sleeves wore dingy braid. A strap around his neck held a pair of binoculars that rested against his chest.

"Now then, Phillips," said the old man, "what does the wireless tell us?"

"Very little, Captain Smith," said Phillips. "Nothing at all, in fact."

"But this lad can tell you," said Kemish.

"Who's this lad?" asked the captain. "Your name, son? I haven't seen you before, have I? Where have you been?"

"His name's Tyler," said Kemish. "He walked out from the land. I found him outside boiler room four."

"Tyler," said the captain, turning to him, "you walked across the ocean floor to our ship? You're not one of our spirits, then?"

"No," said Tyler.

"And what's this? A dog? Do I know this dog?"

"That's Spoofer," said Tyler. "He's my dog. Spoofer and I walked for hours."

"And the sea? Where was the sea while

you did all this walking?" asked the captain.

"Well, actually, my sister, her name's Anna, she poured it in this hole," said Tyler. "Spoofer dug this hole in the beach, and she carried buckets of water and kept on pouring it in this hole Spoofer dug."

"All the sea?" said the captain. "The entire ocean? Every drop of it?"

"Well, I think just about," said Tyler. "We did see some puddles and little ponds along the way."

"And this sister of yours, this Anna," said the captain. "How old is she?"

"Four," said Tyler. "Well, actually, four going on five. She'll be five next month."

The captain took his binoculars and gave them to Tyler. "Put these to your eyes, lad," he said, "and take a sweep out there to the east. Out there where that glimmer of daylight is showing."

Tyler peered through the binoculars. At first, in the beginning light of dawn, he saw the ocean floor sloping gently downward. Then he raised the binoculars a little. Now he saw bright lights flickering far away in the distance. He studied them a moment, swinging the binoculars first to his right, then to his left. What were they? Now he saw. They were ships, great ships, many of them, floating in a wide, wide ocean.

"But there wasn't any more to dip up," said Tyler. He handed the binoculars back to the captain. "She poured it all in the hole so I could walk out here."

"She knew you were coming here?" asked the captain.

"Well," said Tyler, "I told her she couldn't really pour all the ocean in that hole. And she said, yes she could. And I said, 'Well, if you can do that, I can walk to the *Titanic.*' It's my favorite place in the whole world."

"So you did," said the captain. "Or so you thought you did. But you see, Tyler lad, the *Titanic* rests on the edge of the continental shelf."

"Two and a half miles down we are," said Kemish. "Right, Captain?"

"Aye," said the captain. "But the Atlantic goes seven miles deep where it wants to, out there, beyond the continental shelf. That's more sea than you *and* your sister could dip up in a lifetime, Tyler lad."

"It's not only the ships you might have left high and dry," said wireless operator Phillips. "Think of the fish. The whales, the sharks, the dolphins, the sole and bass and tuna. There's so many of them. Must be a bit crowded out there now. Those millions of fish. Swimming around. Bumping into each other. All those lobsters and crabs wondering why they can't swim home."

"I didn't mean to hurt them," said Tyler.

"Of course you didn't," said the captain. "But we don't always manage to do what we set out to do. Sometimes we do something we didn't mean to do."

"Did you ever do something you didn't mean to do?" asked Tyler.

"You're standing aboard it," said the captain. "Eh, Phillips? Right, Kemish?"

The men nodded. Neither said a word.

"You have to think things through, Tyler lad," said the captain. "You have to say to yourself, 'If I do this or that, what happens then?'"

The captain paused. "I'll put it another way, lad. You have to think, 'If I encourage my little sister to pour the ocean into a hole in the beach, what happens then?'"

The captain peered through the binoculars toward the distant ships. With the sky glowing pink in the sunrise, Tyler could now make out the ships far off in the distance. Their lights still flickered. The captain lowered the binoculars. He looked at Tyler. He glanced from Kemish to Phillips. Now his eyes came back to Tyler. And now he peered through the binoculars again.

At last he dropped them to his chest. He leaned toward Tyler. His voice was soft. "We didn't think things through," he said. "Watertight bulkheads. A splendid idea. But nobody thought about what might happen if we didn't seal them off at the top. Nobody said, 'What if some fill up at the bow and the bow tips down? And the sea cascades from one compartment into another. What about that?'" The captain shook his head, his chin down. "We didn't think it through."

Kemish and Phillips had turned away from the captain. "It's all right, men," he said. "Back to your posts. I'll chat with the lad awhile. Here, Tyler, come into the wheelhouse."

CHAPTER 8

Discovering the Dogs

THE CAPTAIN TURNED to the wall at his back. It was low, with a gap above it, running across the sloping deck. The wheelhouse roof sagged above it, high here and low there, all broken down and clumsy at the far end. The captain stepped into the wall. He dissolved from the chest down, but his head and shoulders stayed clear and solid in the space above it. "Come along, lad," he called.

"I can't do that," said Tyler.

"Oh. My, my," said the captain. "I don't suppose you can." He stepped back toward Tyler. "Come along to the hatch at the end."

The captain had to tug hard at a door that was built like a shutter. It creaked as he opened it.

Spoofer barked. He stepped back, his tail straight up. He barked and barked, crouching down on his front paws.

Tyler heard a yipping and a yapping from the far end of the wheelhouse. Spoofer, barking furiously, ran down there. He backed away, barked, stepped forward, then backed away. Tyler could see a big dog with stiff, straight hair. It was dissolving through the wheelhouse wall. Right behind it appeared a small dog with a little round face and pushed-in nose.

"All right, there, Kitty," said Captain Smith. "That's enough. You, too, Sun."

The three dogs stopped barking and began sniffing.

"Are they your dogs?" asked Tyler. Spoofer was down on his front paws, his tail swishing back and forth in the air. He jumped up and ran playfully around the sloping deck. Both of the other dogs joined in the chase.

"In a manner of speaking, they're mine," said the captain. "They've been with me for a long time."

"They belonged to a passenger?" asked Tyler.

"Two passengers," said the captain. "The Airedale, that's Kitty, belonged to a gentleman named John Jacob Astor. And the little Pekingese is called Sun Yat-sen. His owner was Henry Sleeper Harper. I think he published books."

Tyler looked at the captain. The dogs had run around the corner of the wheelhouse toward the wireless shack. The captain held the hatch shutter open. "I think I sense some question on your face, Tyler lad," he said as Tyler went ahead of him into the wheelhouse. "Out with it."

"Well, are the dogs . . . "

"Spirits?" said the captain. "Oh my, yes."

"Like you and fireman Kemish and wireless operator Phillips?" asked Tyler.

"Yes. But we're not all quite alike," said the captain. "Some aboard ship are survivors."

"Survivors?"

"Survivors. Rescued," said the captain.

"And their spirits are here? On the wreck of the *Titanic*?" said Tyler.

"A few. A handful," said the captain. "Survivors. Rescued."

"But they're all spirits?" asked Tyler. "How come they're here?"

"They wanted it," said the captain. "You see, after the rescue, they lived their lives. And when the time came, some had lived long lives, they wanted to come back."

"They wanted to be here?" asked Tyler. "On the wreck? Forever?"

"As did I." The captain nodded. He swung his hip up onto a tall stool beside the ship's wheel, squirming his way into a comfortable position. He clapped his open hand down on his knee. "She is my ship, you know. I went down with her. I belong here."

"But the others. Phillips. He's wearing a life jacket," said Tyler. "How come he's wearing a life jacket?"

"Devotion to duty," said the captain. "Phillips sat in the wireless shack and wouldn't move. He cracked out messages into the night. All those three hours. First the CQD. That was the international distress code, you know. Then the SOS. We were the first ever to send the SOS. Did you know that?"

Tyler nodded. "But he had his life jacket on?"

"No," said the captain. "The second operator, operator Bride, strapped it onto him while Phillips kept working the telegraph key. Phillips wouldn't be budged."

The captain paused. He gazed beyond Tyler, out beyond the wheelhouse, where the pink sky was turning to blue. A shaft of light from the rising sun caught his white beard. "Such devotion," he muttered.

He took a deep breath and turned back

to Tyler. "When the power became weak and the last lifeboat was gone, I ordered him off. I told them all, the whole crew, whoever could hear me, 'You've done your duty, boys. Now, every man for himself.' And just then, a stoker, up from the bottom deck, sneaked up on Phillips." The captain paused to let Tyler think about what happened.

"He sneaked up on Phillips, this man from the bowels of the ship did, while Phillips was still at his telegraph key," the captain went on. "And he tried to take the jacket off Phillips."

"He did?" said Tyler.

"He did."

"What did Phillips do?" asked Tyler.

"He and Bride took care of him," said the captain. "They landed a punch or two. I heard about it before we went down."

The captain paused again. "Tyler, Phillips was committed. The man did his job. He brought the rescue ships. So after his long life, when his spirit wanted to come aboard, life jacket and all, he was more than welcome. We have to be grateful to the people who do the job."

"And Kemish?" said Tyler. "What made him want to come back?"

"Kemish worked the boiler rooms. He had sweated in the boiler room of many a ship and he knew boiler rooms that were hotter than the open door of a chimney in hell. And he found the *Titanic* clean and fresh and new. She wasn't like the old tubs he'd stoked. On this ship, he was in heaven. His spirit couldn't ask for anything more comfortable."

"But the dogs?" said Tyler. "They wanted to be here, too?"

"Funny thing about dogs," said the captain. "They have their ways. Kitty, there. She went down with us. Her master went down, you know. Colonel Astor. First-class passage, he had. But he stood back from the lifeboats. Gave up his chance. And the dog stuck by him."

"And Sun Yat-sen?"

The captain sighed. "Well, that's where the little lap-dog had the advantage. He was in first class, too. And Mr. Harper just scooped him up in his arms. Took him right along in the lifeboat."

The captain paused. He smiled at Tyler. "Just a few years went by," he said, "and one day, there was Sun Yat-sen, chasing Kitty up and down the deck. I must say, having the two of them has been a joy."

He lifted his cap and ran his hand back through his white hair. He rubbed his eyes. "Well now," he said. "I know a lad who must be hungry after that long walk. Breakfast, then?"

The captain reached out. Tyler saw a large brass bell. He had not noticed it before. Had it been there all along? Or had it just appeared as the captain reached out?

The captain grabbed a piece of rope that hung down from the bell's ringer. He snapped it sideways. The bell clanged.

CHAPTER 9

Meeting the Kids

A FIGURE APPEARED, dissolving through the battered wall of the wheelhouse. It was a man dressed all in white. He wore a round white cap with a wide band but no peak. His white jacket was topped by a high collar. A wide flap buttoned against his right shoulder. The jacket was long, dropping to the man's knees. As he took a step toward them, Tyler could see the bottoms of the man's white pants brushing little puffs of white dust from his white shoes.

"Morning, captain," said the man.

"Sticky buns this morning?" asked the captain.

"Of course," said the man. "Piping hot this very minute."

The captain turned to Tyler. "You like sticky buns, lad?"

Tyler grinned. He couldn't help himself. He loved sticky buns.

"Well, Tyler," said the captain. "You're in luck. This is chief night baker Belford. He knows a thing or two about sticky buns. And about dining first class."

The captain turned back to the baker. "We have a visitor. Young Tyler, here. I think a bit of breakfast would be in order. Then, Tyler, I think you'd best be on your way back home. And you'd best manage some way to put the sea back where it belongs."

"Tyler lad," said baker Belford. "Did you bring a dog along?"

"You've seen the dog?" asked the captain.

"Racing about the decks with Kitty and Sun Yat-sen," said the baker. "Had me wondering. I'd never seen that third dog before. Well, come along, lad. Sticky buns and cocoa. That's Master Dodge's favorite." He turned and began to dissolve through the wall where he had first appeared.

"I can't go that way," called Tyler.

"Hold on, Belford," said the captain. "The boy's not a spirit. Try the hatch, there."

The baker returned. Tyler followed him onto the sloping deck. He had to hurry to keep up with the slim white figure. "Who's Master Dodge?" Tyler called. "Is he the ship's master?"

"Not likely," said the baker. "No. He's Master Washington Dodge. A first-class passenger he was. An American lad, like you."

"Why do you call him master?"

"Ah well, that is what fine young lads like you and he were called in 1912."

They quickly reached a huge room filled with metal tables. Along the wall to the left stood a row of stoves with great

hoods hanging above them. Large pots
and pans were piled everywhere atop the
stoves. They had great blobs of rust
growing on them. Some were brown.
Some were orange.

Chief night baker Belford hurried to
one of the stoves. It was different. It
looked clean and shiny. The pots and pans
sitting on it gleamed brightly. He pulled
open the oven door. He grabbed a giant
pair of mittens and reached inside. Out
came a baking sheet. On it were rows and
rows of sticky buns.

"Stickies!" he yelled suddenly. "Sticky
buns! Who's ready for sticky buns?"

Behind the baker, Tyler saw a big round
table with chairs. And quickly dissolving
into view were three children who were
just scrambling onto the chairs. "Sticky
buns!" they cried together. "Come on!"

"Belford's beautiful buns!" yelled a
small boy. His shirt had a broad white
collar that overlapped his brown tweed
jacket. Tweed straps ran over each
shoulder. They went down to a tweed belt

round his waist. His trousers were gathered just below the knee. Big brass buttons kept them tight above his long brown stockings.

"Big bountiful bouncy buns by Belford!" cried an older boy as he settled in his chair. His trousers were shaped the same way at the knee but were made of corduroy. He wore a brown knit sweater, a white shirt, and a bright red necktie.

"Oh, Frankie, stop it," said a girl wearing a dark blue dress that hung to her knees. It had a wide collar across her shoulders, with white trim like a sailor's shirt. Her long blond hair was twisted in two braids down her back. Each braid ended with a white ribbon bow.

"Now then," said chief night baker Belford. "I want some attention. We have a visitor. This is Tyler. He's just come aboard."

"Just in time for breakfast," cried the boy in corduroy.

"For sticky buns!" yelled the little boy in the big white collar. "And cocoa!"

"All right, Master Dodge," said Belford. "You'll have your cocoa." He turned to Tyler. "This is Washington Dodge. He's our youngest. Likes his cocoa."

"We all like cocoa," said the girl.

"And sticky buns," said the boy in corduroy.

Belford was busy now, serving the buns onto fine china plates. "Here, Tyler," he said, handing Tyler a plate. "Careful. It's rather hot. Sit right here."

The baker pulled a chair out from the table to help Tyler get seated. Tyler parked his boom box on the chair beside him.

"Yes," said Belford, "he likes his cocoa. First thing aboard the *Carpathia*, when they offered him coffee, he said he'd like cocoa."

"I said I'd prefer to have cocoa, thank you," said Dodge. "I remembered my please-and-thank-you."

"He isn't always such a goody," said the girl.

Belford was going from one to another,

pouring cocoa into big round cups. Tyler saw that each saucer had the letters W.S.L. So did each plate with a sticky bun. "Who's W.S.L.?" he asked.

"White Star Line," said the boy in corduroy. "Well, Tyler, my name's Frankie. Frankie Goldsmith. What's in the black case?"

"I'm sorry," Belford was saying. "I got busy. I forgot to say who each of you is. Now this young lady dressed like a sailor is Eva Hart."

Eva jumped from her chair. She caught the edge of her skirt with each hand and quickly made a deep curtsy toward Tyler. "Yes, what *is* that thing?"

"It's my boom box," said Tyler.

"Let's see it," said Frankie, jumping up and coming around the table.

CHAPTER 10

Playing the CD

THEY GATHERED AROUND TYLER. He un-plugged the earphones, letting them hang around his neck, and turned on the boom box. The sound swelled up into the great room. Frankie and Eva stepped back. Washington Dodge stuck his fingers in his ears.

Eva began to move to the music. "What *is* that?" she asked. "I *love* it."

"It's the *Titanic* music," said Tyler.

Now Frankie caught the pulse of the music. He began to sway to it and made small steps to the steady beat. He circled around Eva as she danced slowly toward the boom box. "The *Titanic* music?" she asked.

"Our music went down with the ship," said baker Belford. "Those men played their hearts out."

"But this is different," said Eva. "They never played anything like this. I couldn't dance to what they played then."

"I'm playing my CD," said Tyler. "In the boom box."

"Your CD?" said Eva. "What's a CD?'

"It's a record," said Tyler. "A compact disk. CD stands for compact disk."

"See?" said Frankie. "He can carry it around while it plays. Must be another of Edison's inventions."

A voice interrupted him. "All right, children. Had your sticky buns, eh?" Suddenly the figure of Captain Smith dissolved into place standing beside baker Belford.

Frankie and Eva stopped dancing.

"Best turn off the boom box, Tyler lad," said the captain. "Best get under way. Big day ahead of you."

"Big day?" said Tyler.

"Well, if you're going to pump the Atlantic back from wherever your little sister drained it," said the captain. "We need the sea, lad. You've had your bit of sport, eh?"

The captain clapped his hands once. Frankie dissolved away through the table where they had been sitting. The captain clapped again. Eva was gone.

Washington Dodge was standing beside the boom box as it sat on the chair. He pushed a button on it. The music stopped. "Well done, Master Dodge," said the captain. He clapped his hands again. Dodge dissolved, ever so slowly, as if he wished he could stay.

"That boy," said Captain Smith. "He's got us all charmed."

"Why?" said Tyler. "Why is he here? Why are they all here?"

The captain pulled out a chair from the table and sat down. "I say, Belford," he called, "I'll try one of those buns. And a spot of cocoa."

He turned back to Tyler. "They wanted to come back," he went on. "They lived their lives. But nothing seemed as important as the *Titanic*, I expect. Take young Dodge, there."

"What did he do?" asked Tyler. "When he was grown, I mean?"

"Stocks and bonds," said the captain as Belford set down a sticky bun on a W.S.L. plate and poured him a cup of cocoa. "Money. His life was all Park Avenue and Wall Street. Couldn't match the rescue and the fun he had aboard the *Carpathia*, I suppose."

"He thought it was fun?" said Tyler.

"I expect it was rather an adventure for a lad that young," said the captain. "Traveling first class and all that."

He paused to bite into his sticky bun. Chewing, he called out, "Best ever, Belford! I don't know how you do it!"

The captain sipped his cocoa. He gazed at the sticky bun on his plate. He thought for a moment, then spoke again. "Those hours in the lifeboat with his Mum.

Hauled up in a mail sack. Dumped out on the *Carpathia*'s deck. The cocoa."

The captain chuckled to himself as he took another bite. "The lad spots his Dad. Sees him in the crowd of survivors. He'd come aboard from another lifeboat. And the lad not only doesn't tell his Mum. He goes and hides from his Dad. So neither Mum nor Dad knows the other one is alive."

The captain picked up his cup. About to take a sip, he peered over the top of it. "Would you spoof your Mum and Dad that way? At a time like that?"

"Spoofer!" said Tyler. "Where did Spoofer go?"

"He's fine," said the captain. "Sound asleep in the wheelhouse, with the other two. They all wore each other out."

The captain set down his empty cup. "Years of numbers, Tyler lad," he said. "Young Dodge spent years looking at numbers. Not much adventure there. I couldn't have done it. Doubt if you could. I went to sea. And look at you."

"Me?" said Tyler.

"Well, here you are," said Captain Smith, "out here at the edge of the continental shelf. I'd call that adventure. You have a spirit that has brought you here."

"And Master Dodge's spirit wanted to come back here?" said Tyler. "After his whole life?"

The captain stood up. "Exactly. So back he came. We were delighted. He's a bit of a tease, you know. Leads young Eva a merry chase."

The captain rubbed his hands. He lifted his cap and ran a hand through his white hair. "Come along, now. Let's find your dog and set you on your way." He started toward the deck outside the galley.

CHAPTER 11

Beating Down Demons

TYLER RAN AFTER THE CAPTAIN. "Tell me about Eva," he said. "What made her come back?"

The captain stopped and looked down at Tyler. "Eva," he said. He shook his head. "Eva, Eva." He gazed along the deck. He lifted his binoculars to his eyes. Slowly he turned, looking along the far-off horizon in the morning light.

Then he let the binoculars drop to his chest again. "That little girl," he said. "Her life went on for 84 years before she came back to us."

The captain squatted down to Tyler as

if telling him a secret. "All that time," he said softly, "her spirit was drawing back to us. Do you know, lad, for 16 years after we went down, that girl had nightmares?"

"Nightmares?" said Tyler.

"Oh, yes. Nightmares." The captain stood up and walked along. "The girl couldn't sleep. But she found a way to beat down her demons."

"Her demons?" said Tyler. "What were her demons?"

"Her memories. Her bad dreams," said the captain. "The sight of our great ship standing on her bow. The lifeboats. The screams. The terrible sounds. And the terrible silence. The night, then. The boats alone under the stars. She took charge. One has to do that, you know, Tyler lad. One has to do that."

"How?" asked Tyler. "How did she take charge?"

"Returned to sea," said the captain. "Sixteen years after she was rescued, she booked passage across the Atlantic, she did. Made herself do it."

"And that stopped her bad dreams?" said Tyler.

"It took more than that." The captain stood still. He turned to Tyler, looking down at him.

Again he seemed to share a secret. He spoke softly. "Here she was," he said. "Aboard ship. A fine Atlantic vessel. And she locked herself in her cabin. Just bring me food and drink, she said, and I'll stay here and beat down my demons."

"For four days?" said Tyler.

"Four glorious days at sea," said the captain as he turned and walked on. "Never once came out on deck."

"And the nightmares?" said Tyler. "Didn't she have more bad dreams?"

"Not one," said the captain. "Not for the rest of her life, another 68 years. Eva did what one has to do. She let her demons know she was in charge. We had to reward that spirit. She had such a strong connection with us. We made her welcome."

They were back at the wheelhouse. The captain opened the shutter hatch. There were the three dogs, sound asleep. Spoofer was curled up in a tight ball, his nose under his tail. Kitty lay flat on her belly, her chin between her forepaws on the deck. Sun Yat-sen lay on her side, leaning back against Kitty.

"Well, then, lad," said the captain. "I think we must see you on your way."

"But what about Frankie?" said Tyler. "You haven't told me about him. Did he have a strong connection, too?"

Spoofer's head came up. He looked at Tyler. He tilted his head, so one ear hung down to the side. He always looked that way when he was puzzled. Then he flapped his tail once on the deck and snuggled down again.

"Frankie," said the captain. "Yes. Well, let's see. Step out on the bridge."

Tyler followed the captain out onto the bridge. Waving his arm, the captain motioned toward the bow of the wrecked ship. "There," he said. "See him? On the forecastle. Just beyond that big square shape that's rather flattened."

Tyler saw him. Frankie was just ducking down behind the shape. His head came up. He ducked down again.

"Is he hiding?" asked Tyler.

"Hide and seek," said the captain. "Plays it with some of our cabin boys. His favorite game."

"I haven't seen any cabin boys," said Tyler.

"You may," said the captain. He paused. "And you may not. Frankie sees them. He tells me he remembers them well. He was in a lifeboat, and it was being lowered to the sea. They passed a porthole as they went. Frankie looked in and there the cabin boys were. Playing hide and seek. I suppose Frankie was just your age."

"And he wanted to come back and play hide and seek."

"I think," said the captain slowly, "Frankie just missed his father so. He and his Mum were rescued. His Pop, no. His Pop said good-bye and watched them go. And for 70 years Frankie had the April funk."

"The April funk?" said Tyler.

"A blue funk. A mood," said the captain. "Couldn't shake it. Middle of April, everything stood still. For Frankie, life just stopped. Never got over it."

"You mean he just didn't do anything?" said Tyler.

"Sometimes not for days," said the captain. "Couldn't let go. Wanted to hold onto the memory."

Captain Smith turned back toward the wheelhouse. "We have to let go, lad. Have to let go. We can't live on memories. Some try to. But it seldom works."

CHAPTER 12

Following the Dogs

THEY WERE BACK INSIDE the wheelhouse. The captain clanged his bell. The dogs jumped up. They all shuddered, shaking their coats. Spoofer stood before Tyler and wagged his tail.

"He's ready to hike," said the captain.

"I don't want to go," said Tyler.

The captain stared down at him. He said nothing.

"I want to play hide-and-seek with Frankie," said Tyler. "And Eva and Washington."

"No," said the captain firmly.

"And the cabin boys," said Tyler. "You said Frankie is playing with the cabin boys. Why can't I?"

"I said no," repeated the captain even more firmly.

"Why not?" asked Tyler.

"Well, lad," said the captain softly, "there's a line I cannot let you cross."

"A line?" said Tyler.

"You can't see it," the captain went on, "but it's there." He rubbed his hands together as if that was the end of that. He looked at Tyler for a long moment.

Then he spoke. "You've had your play," the captain said. "Now you have to put the sea back where it belongs. Off you go."

The captain turned to the hatch. "Spoofer!" he called. "Come along, Tyler lad."

Tyler picked up his boom box. Spoofer jumped up and down at his feet, then ran around him twice. The captain led them onto the bridge, then went around the corner to the sloping deck. He stopped.

Turning back toward the bridge, he put two fingers in his mouth and whistled the loudest whistle Tyler had ever heard.

Kitty and Sun Yat-sen romped past them. They scampered away along the deck. Spoofer ran after them.

"They'll show the way!" called the captain. "Just follow them, lad. They know the way ashore."

Tyler hurried after them. At the grand staircase, the three dogs were standing at the first step. Panting, they looked back at Tyler. When he reached them, they turned and darted down the stairs.

Down they all went. Past the great hallways with their flickering lights. Past crumpled tables and chairs. Past broken china. Past giant paintings hanging in torn shreds from splintered frames. And down stairway after stairway, all tipped this way and that so it was hard to hurry down them.

At last the dogs ran through a broken doorway crusted with blobs of rust. Out they went onto the sand, yelping and chasing each other. First Kitty was in front, then Spoofer ran past her. Then little Sun Yat-sen went rolling and yip-yapping to the front.

Tyler looked back. The giant wreck stood up against the sky. Off to the right, was that the bridge? He could see something white. The captain's cap? Yes! There he was, in his white uniform. Now he lifted his cap and waved it in the air.

Tyler turned and looked ahead. What was Kitty doing? She had stopped. Her nose was down sniffing the sand. She ran in tight little circles, sniffing, sniffing. She stood still. She began to dig. Her front paws spun faster and faster. The sand flew out behind her. Her nose sank lower and lower into the hole as she dug. Her paws seemed to whirl.

Spoofer ran to where Kitty was digging. He sniffed at the hole in the sand. He ran ahead, nose to sand as he went sniffing along. Then he stopped and began to dig.

Little Sun Yat-sen scampered to Spoofer. He sniffed. He tossed his head, jumped right up in the air and ran along sniffing. Now he, too, was digging.

What was Tyler hearing? Not the boom box. Another sound. He turned down the boom box. He could hear gurgling. Bubbling. Gushing.

From the hole where Kitty was digging, a fountain of bubbling green and white water burst upward. It sprayed into the air, glorious and white and sparkling with joy. Kitty jumped back. She crouched down and looked at the fountain of spray, her tail straight up and wagging happily.

Another fountain burst where Spoofer was digging. And now Sun Yat-sen's digging brought another plume of water climbing high in the sky.

Spoofer ran ahead of them and dug as fast as he could. Instantly another fountain burst from the sand. A giant geyser shot far, far into the sky above them. It was like when Tyler's teacher showed the video of Old Faithful in Yellowstone Park. The water just went up sky-high. The spray began to fall on him like rain. It felt clean and cool. The air was fresh and good.

Clang! Clang-clang-clang!

Tyler looked back at the wreck. The captain's bell. He knew it. He could just see the captain's white figure standing on the bridge. Was he putting his hand to his mouth?

The whistle! The loudest whistle Tyler ever heard whistled! It almost hurt his ears, as far from the wreck as he was. He looked around to see what the dogs were doing.

Kitty and Sun Yat-sen had stopped in their tracks. Their heads were turned, looking back toward the ship. The water was shooting upward beside them. For just a moment they seemed frozen there.

But Spoofer was already far ahead of them. He was digging as fast as he could. He did not stop. Had he heard the whistle?

Kitty and Sun Yat-sen turned toward the ship. Off they went, the big dog galloping over the sand and little Sun's paws almost invisible as he raced after her. In a few seconds, they had disappeared in the distance.

Tyler hurried toward Spoofer. Where he dug, another plume of white water streamed straight up in front of the dog. For a second, he disappeared. But now he came dashing from behind the giant fountain and again ran ahead of Tyler. And again his paws spun in the sand.

Tyler looked back. As far back as he could see, the fountains were still shooting into the air. Some sent the water steadily upward in a tight stream. Some were thick white geysers of spray. Some were gentle low fountains that sprinkled constantly in a wide circle. Above them all, a giant rainbow arched across the sky.

There went Spoofer lickety-split, dashing ahead, leaping and running across the sand. Fountains were bursting into the air in all directions. One after another they appeared. Great columns of water shooting high into the sky. A forest of fountains.

Tyler ran, swinging his boom box to help speed himself along. He knew he'd better hurry. His feet were splashing in water. Splish-splash, splish-splash, splish-splash.

Water was covering everything. He could see puddles growing into ponds. He had to run around ponds that were fast becoming lakes. And still Spoofer ran ahead, stopped to dig, darted around another fresh fountain, ran on, dug, ducked under the spray.

What was this? Here, beside this lake. Just at the edge of the water. The water was rippling toward it. Gentle waves were lapping around it. A small boat. Old. Beat-up.

Tyler was wading now. He splashed toward the boat. As he got to it, the water around it grew deep enough to lift it from the sand. He grabbed hold, setting his boom box on the seat near the bow. He climbed in. The boat floated along, drifting from the push he gave getting in.

Tyler looked for oars. He found none. The boat drifted in and out of the spray from the fountains and geysers. Where was Spoofer?

There he was, splashing toward the boat. "C'mon, Spoof!" yelled Tyler. "Here, Spoof! Attaboy, come on!"

Spoofer was swimming. Tyler reached out and grabbed the dog's front paws, pulling him aboard. Spoofer jumped up onto the small seat in the bow of the boat.

"Watch the boom box!" cried Tyler. He reached for it and grabbed it. He turned away to protect it just as Spoofer shuddered and shook himself, spraying water everywhere.

"Okay, down here, boy," said Tyler, patting the bottom of the boat. Spoofer jumped down from the seat and curled up at Tyler's feet.

Tyler looked around. Behind him, toward the stern of the boat, lay an old piece of canvas. It looked like a big torn bag.

The spray from the fountains was stronger and stronger and wetter and wetter. Tyler put his boom box down beside Spoofer. He lay down beside his dog and pulled the old torn canvas over them. It just covered Spoofer and the boom box and most of himself.

CHAPTER 13

Facing the Crowd

THE SUN WAS STARTING TO CLIMB up out of the ocean and into the sky in the east. Tyler rubbed his eyes. He heard voices far away. Was his boom box on? No. The voices seemed louder. Spoofer sat up. He cocked his head to one side so one ear hung down.

Tyler looked around. The boat was high and dry on the beach. Spoofer jumped out. He dashed down the beach to the surf and ran back. Off he went again, kicking the light sand as he frolicked along.

Suddenly Spoofer came running back. Behind him people were running. "That's it!" someone yelled. "That's the dog! That's Spoofer! And there's the boy! There he is!"

Now Tyler was at the center of a crowd. Everybody was hugging him and kissing him. Faces he didn't know were laughing and crying. There was his father, with Anna in his arms. He put Anna down on the sand. Dad was picking up Tyler. His mother was hugging him. His father was laughing. His mother was crying. Anna was grinning. Then his father was crying and his mother was laughing.

At last Tyler's father set him down on his feet. "Just let me look at you," he said as he wiped the tears from his eyes.

He squatted down. His face was level with Tyler's face. "Hey, Tyler," he said, with a puzzled look. "Where did you get those great big old-fashioned earphones?"

"Well, actually," said Tyler, "first wireless operator Phillips gave them to me."

AUTHOR'S NOTE ON SOURCES

Eva Hart

Eva Hart died at 91 in 1996. She had never married. Until late in life, she chose not to talk about the disaster. But in 1993, when she was 88, she agreed to be interviewed about what she experienced at the age of seven. "I saw that ship sink," she said. "I never closed my eyes. I didn't sleep at all. I saw it. I heard it, and nobody could possibly forget it. I can remember the colors, the sounds, everything. The worst thing I can remember are the screams." Yet even worse, she added, was what followed: "It seemed as if once everybody had gone, drowned, finished, the whole world was standing still. There was nothing, just this deathly, terrible silence in the dark night with the stars overhead." According to her obituary in *The New York Times* (February 16, 1996), "Miss Hart was plagued with nightmares until, after her mother's death when she was 23, she confronted her fears head on, returning to sea and locking herself in a cabin for four days until the nightmares went away."

Frankie Goldsmith

Frank Goldsmith often talked of how, when he was nine years old, "as his descending lifeboat passed a porthole, he saw teen-age crew members playing hide and seek" and how "the *Titanic* shot off rockets as if it were the King's birthday." Throughout his lifetime, in April he became eerily quiet, saying only a few words in several days. After his death at 79, his family met his request by arranging for his ashes to be dropped into the Atlantic ocean some 1,200 miles northeast of New York City by Petty Officer John Flynn and the crew of a U.S. Coast Guard reconnaissance plane. (*The New York Times*, April 16, 1982.)

Master Washington Dodge, Jr.

Washington Dodge, Jr., was not quite five years old when he was hauled aboard the *Carpathia* in a mail sack. Offered coffee by a steward, he declared his preference for cocoa and was promptly fetched some. Later he saw his father come aboard from a lifeboat but "decided it would be great fun" to keep the news to himself rather than inform his mother, with whom he had shared an earlier boat. An hour passed before his parents found each other, but "I wasn't scolded," he recalled. Interviewed in 1962, when he was 55, Dodge recalled how he had been frightened by the hissing roar as steam escaped from the sinking ship's boilers. "It's the kind of noise I still dislike to this day," he said. (Walter Lord, *A Night to Remember*, New York: Henry Holt, 1955; *The New York Times*, April 15, 1962.)

Fireman Kemish and First Wireless Operator Phillips
Fireman George Kemish and First Wireless Operator John George Phillips were interviewed by Walter Lord as he wrote his classic book on the *Titanic*. Kemish remembered what an improvement the *Titanic*'s boiler rooms were, compared to earlier ships on which he had sailed. The *Titanic*, he said, was "a good job . . . not what we were accustomed to in old ships, slogging our guts out and nearly roasted by the heat."
Lord described the attempted theft of the radioman's life jacket. Wireless Operator Phillips recalled how he was tapping out the international distress signal "CQD" when Second Wireless Operator Harold Bride suggested, "Send SOS. It's the new call, and it may be your last chance to send

it." Laughing at the joke, he said, at 12:45 a.m. he sent the first SOS in history.

Kitty and Sun Yat-sen

Lord noted that first-class passenger Henry Sleeper Harper took his Pekingese, Sun Yat-sen, with him in the lifeboat rescued by the *Carpathia*. And he reported that John Jacob Astor's Airedale, Kitty, was among the *Titanic*'s first-class passengers.

Night Chief Baker Belford

At 92, Night Chief Baker Walter Belford was present in 1962 to commemorate the 50th anniversary of the disaster. He recalled the moment when the *Titanic* hit the iceberg: "We were working on the fifth deck amidships, baking for the next day. There was a shudder all through the ship about 11:40 p.m. The provisions came tumbling down and the oven doors came open." He described his strongest recollection: The scene on the bridge as Captain Edward J. Smith stood staunchly waiting for his ship to sink. Belford still recalled the words of Captain Smith as he dismissed a group of crewmen: "Well, boys, I've done the best I can for you. Now it's in your own hands. Do the best you can to save yourselves." Wearing his baker's white uniform, Belford said, he "went over the side straight away. I jumped overboard from the well deck about thirty feet above the water." Also attending the 50th anniversary ceremony was stockbroker Washington Dodge, Jr. (*The New York Times* and *The New York Herald Tribune,* April 16, 1962; *The New York Times,* April 15, 1962.)

The bright brass on the continental shelf
The *Titanic*'s position on the edge of the continental shelf was reported in *The New York Times* on July 31, 1986. A front-page photo caption noted a "railing and brass-trimmed porthole . . . The brass is kept polished by swift currents along the ocean floor." The news story, reporting on 11 dives to the wreck by an expedition led by Dr. Robert D. Ballard of the Woods Hole Oceanographic Institution, described how "the hull is covered with streams of rust hanging like rusty icicles, some almost complete over portholes and windows."

TITANIC FACTS

Timeline

1907 In London, England, J. Bruce Ismay, managing director of the White Star Line of passenger ships, and Lord William James Pirrie, chairman of shipbuilders Harland and Wolff, first discuss plans to build the world's largest ship.

1908 *July 29,* At the Harland and Wolff shipyard in Belfast, Ireland, plans for the *Titanic* are reviewed.

1909 *March,* the keel of the *Titanic* is laid.

1911 *May 31,* The *Titanic* is launched at Belfast.

1912 *April 1,* the *Titanic* completes trials at sea.

April 3, arrives at Southampton to load supplies and passengers for maiden voyage.

April 10, 12:00 noon, sails from Southampton dock.

7:00 p.m., arrives at Cherbourg, France, to board more passengers.

9:00 p.m., sails from Cherbourg.

April 11, 12:30 p.m., arrives at Queenstown, Ireland, to board more passengers and mail.

2:00 p.m., sails from Queenstown for New York.

April 14, 11:40 p.m., strikes iceberg.

April 15, 12:05 a.m., crew is ordered to uncover lifeboats and assemble passengers.

12:15 a.m., first message by wireless radio sends for help.

12:45 a.m., first rocket is launched to signal distress.

12:45 a.m., first lifeboat is lowered.

1:40 a.m., last distress rocket is fired.

2:05 a.m., last lifeboat is lowered.

2:10 a.m., last wireless radio message is sent.

2:18 a.m., ship's lights go out.

2:20 a.m., the *Titanic* sinks.

1985 *September 1,* a search team led by geologist Robert Ballard, using the U.S. Navy's video-based search system, finds the wreckage 450 nautical miles off the Newfoundland coastline at latitude 41° 44' North, longitude 49° 55' West.

Titanic Expeditions

1986 Using a three-person "submersible" and a remote operated vehicle (ROV), Ballard and his crew find the ship lying in two major parts separated by a section of debris 1,800 feet wide.

1987, 1993, 1994, 1996, 1998, and 2000 Expeditions in these years average 21 dives to the wreck, locating or recovering several thousand objects, from massive watertight door gears to fragile perfume vials. Some highlights include:

- Main wheel and steering stand from the wheelhouse at the rear of the ship's bridge;

- Ship's engine telegraph, a mechanical device that relayed instructions about engine speed from the bridge to the engine room, where the noise made it harder to hear verbal orders;

- Automatic whistle timer, which blew the ship's whistle regularly during fog;

- Decorative statue from the Grand Staircase;

- Copper hot water boiler (one of dozens that kept water hot for making fresh tea); and

- Hundreds of miscellaneous candy dishes, demitasse cups, lighting fixtures and chandeliers, fragments of leaded windows, binoculars, pocket watches, and large amounts of passenger baggage.

About the *Titanic*

Size: 46,328 tons total weight. 66,000 tons displacement (the weight of water displaced by the floating ship)

Length: 882.5 feet (equal to four city blocks)

Width: 92.5 feet

Height: 175 feet from keel to tops of four funnels (equal to an 11-story building)

Power: 50,000 horsepower

Speed: 25 knots per hour at full speed ahead

Fuel: 4,427 tons of coal

Some of the provisions: potatoes—40 tons; butter—3 tons; coffee—2,200 pounds; beer and stout—20,000 bottles; mineral water—

15,000 bottles; fresh eggs—40,000; ice cream—1,750 quarts; fresh meat—more than 37 tons; fresh asparagus—800 bundles; lettuce—7,000 heads; flour—250 barrels; sugar—5 tons

Among basic utensils and other supplies: cutlery—44,000 pieces; crockery—57600 items; glassware—29,000 pieces; linens—196,100 items

Lifeboats: 20 (16 wooden, 4 collapsible; only one-third the number to carry all those on board.)

Total number aboard: 2,153

Lives lost: 1,502

Lives saved: 651 (139 crew, 119 men passengers, 393 women and children passengers.)